D1489213

GOODBYE, COOLSVILLE!
HELLO, NERDTOWN!

Concept and Art by:
Tom Bancroft & Rob Corley

Written by:
Jennifer Bancroft

Tommy NELSON

www.tommynelson.com

A Division of Thomas Nelson, Inc.
www.ThomasNelson.com

Text and Illustrations © 2005 Tom Bancroft and Rob Corley
Funnypages Productions, LLC
Jacket and Interior Design: Troy Birdsong
Logo Design: Ron Eddy
www.funnypagesprod.com

Published in Nashville, Tennessee, by Tommy Nelson®, a Division of Thomas Nelson, Inc.

Tommy Nelson® books may be purchased in bulk for educational, business, fundraising, or sales promotional use. For information, please e-mail SpecialMarkets@ThomasNelson.com.

Library of Congress Cataloging-in-Publication Data

Bancroft, Jennifer.
    Goodbye, Coolsville! Hello, Nerdtown!/concept and illustrations by Tom Bancroft and Rob Corley; written by Jennifer Bancroft.
        p. cm. -- (Andi's journal ; bk. 1)
    Summary: Worried about how Andi is adjusting to her mother's death, her father decides they should move from San Francisco to a small town near the Sierra Nevada mountains, where Andi discovers her mother's girlhood journals, makes some new friends, and becomes closer to God.
    ISBN 1-4003-0671-X (soft back)
    1. Moving, Household—Fiction. 2. Christian life—Fiction. 3. Diaries—Fiction. 4. Sierra Nevada (Calif. and Nev.)—Fiction. I. Bancroft, Tom, ill. II. Corley, Rob, ill. III. Title.

    PZ7.B2195Go 2005
    [Fic]—dc22

                                                    2005011329

Printed in China
05 06 07 08 LEO 5 4 3 2 1

Dedicated to our little Andis:
Madison, Alexis, Ansley,
Olivia, Emma, and Ellie.
We pray that you continue
always to seek the Lord
in all that you do.

Table of Contents

Andrea "Andi" Bannerman

1
Just Another Day

ndi Bannerman opened the door to the San Francisco apartment and grabbed her orange jacket from the hook in the hall. It was another drizzly morning in Bay City—hard to believe it was May. Pulling on her jacket and zipping up the collar, Andi took a deep breath of the damp, foggy air. She really didn't mind the thick, cool air that blanketed the city. It gave the city a gloomy look, and that fit her just fine these days.

Walking to school, Andi headed up the hill. The whole place was buzzing with early morning traffic. Honking cars, roaring buses, dinging cable cars, and bellowing fog horns mingled to create quite the soundtrack to accompany Andi's trek to school.

She scrunched down deeper into her jacket and picked up the pace to keep up with the rhythm of the traffic. *Don't be late again this week, no more detentions. Dad would freak. And I've seen enough of that lately to last a while.*

Gaining momentum with each step, Andi decided that she would be detention-free for the remainder of the school year. *How hard can that be? Only four more weeks. I'll just steer clear of trouble, get to school on time. . . . Hey, I'm a good kid. At least I try! And I know I'm not as bad as some of the other kids at that school. Okay, well, maybe people misunderstand me, even say I've got a 'tude . . .*

"Ugh! Whatever!" Andi finally said aloud to stop the rambling in her brain. "Let's just get to school and get this day over with!"

The quad was usually crowded at this time of the morning. Guys gathered on bikes and skateboards. Girls were in clusters of gushes and giggles, sharing every detail of their weekends. Andi deftly moved in and out of the crowd, attempting to reach "the spot," the one on the hill where she and the gang hung out. Abby, Tami, and Jeff were already there chatting and looking the coolest, as always. Sometimes Andi couldn't believe her luck. She was hand-picked to hang out with the cool crowd this year. Andi had never had such status. She still didn't know why they picked her, but she wasn't about to ask either. The hardest part of it all was making sure that she was as cool as they were . . . all the time.

"Hey, guys!"

"Hey, Andi! What's up?"

"Not much."

"Andi, you're in pre-algebra this year, right?"

"Um, yeah," Andi answered.

"Aren't you a little young for that class?" Jeff asked.

Andi stammered, "Uh, well, I dunno." *Oh no. Here it comes! They're gonna find out I'm some kind of brainiac!* "Some computer glitch during registration, I guess," she added coolly.

"Yeah, probably," he answered, looking away from her. He had already lost interest.

Whew! Andi thought. She shook off a shudder. This lying thing was getting to be pretty easy . . . maybe a little too easy.

"Anyway . . ." Jeff turned back to Andi with regained interest, "did you get the homework from Friday?"

"Yup. You missing the assignment? I can look it up for ya."

"No, actually, I just didn't finish it. *Actually*, I didn't even start it." He grinned. "Can I get yours and give it back to you before class?"

Crud! How do I say no to this? How uncool would that be?! Kids are always sharing homework, so technically it wouldn't be cheating. It would just be helping a friend. Yeah, that's it! I'm helping a friend. And that's a good thing, right?! Yeah!

"Sure, Jeff." Andi shrugged. "Just get it back to me before third period, 'kay? Meet me at my locker."

"Cool . . . thanks, Andi."

As Andi handed over the paper, the home-room bell rang. "Well, I'd better go."

2
The Last Straw

A ndi had made it through her first two classes
with ease. In homeroom, Mr. Rogers was full
of news about end-of-the-year activities and
tryouts for various teams for the coming school year.
Andi would have to consider that. Maybe cheering
or volleyball would be fun. She'd talk to Abby. It
wouldn't be fun without a friend.

In science, she was teamed up with the
perfect group for the lab project—dissecting an
earthworm. Her two goofy guy partners were
thrilled. They accomplished the feat with just one
cut. Their enthusiasm meant that Andi didn't have
to touch it at all. But—*ick*—just looking at it made
her want to hurl! It was a good thing she studied the

anatomy at home. She filled in the diagram without poking around at the guts.

When the bell finally rang, a certain urgency took over. *Oh no! I've gotta meet Jeff,* Andi remembered.

Andi took one last look in her locker mirror. Satisfied, she grabbed her pre-algebra book and slammed the locker shut. *Where is he?! I've got to go!* She looked around, hoping to see him sliding around the corner any second. *I can't be late. No detentions, Andi.* Suddenly, a heavy gong of a bell echoed throughout

the hallway. *Warning bell! One more minute!*

"Hey, Holly," Andi called, trying to remain cool, "have you seen Jeff?"

"Not today," the girl replied and hurried away to catch a closing classroom door.

Why does this always happen to me? I was trying to do something nice. Well, sorta. But why can't I slide by just once?

Andi took the stairs two at a time, arriving in the doorway of her math class completely breathless.

The second bell rang. Not in her seat and technically tardy, Andi quickly developed a strategy. *You can do this, Andi. Get it together. You're cool . . . remember, cooool.*

Andi hoped no one would notice her sweaty brow and flushed cheeks. She slowly sauntered to her seat, attempting to not be the last kid standing in the room.

"Good morning, Miss Bannerman." Mr. Wise looked over his glasses at Andi.

That's it. I'm dead. "Morning," she squeaked.

"Do you have something for me, Andi?"

"I'm not sure, sir."

"Not sure? How could you not be sure about that?" Mr. Wise said sternly.

Andi was definitely in trouble; she just wasn't sure why. Mr. Wise normally overlooked slight tardiness. Other kids were still milling around. Why was he picking on her?

"Andi, read the board." Mr. Wise watched Andi's expression as she turned to read: "All homework due in the basket immediately."

Trapped, she thought.

"So, Andi, let's try this again. Do you have something for me?"

"Um, I do, sir. . . . I mean, I did, sir. Let me find it."

"Yes, Andi. You find it. We'll wait."

She didn't like the sound of that. Breaking out into a new sweat and silently rejoicing that she did, in fact, wear deodorant, Andi slowly started to leaf through her folder. Reaching the last paper, Andi faked her best look of surprise and met the eyes burning a hole through the top of her head. "Sssir, I seem to have misplaced my homework. B-but I did do it. Maybe I left it at home."

Now, Andi's conscience had kicked in and

was completely killing her. She had helped someone to cheat and then went on to lie about it—all before lunchtime! How much worse could the day get?

"Andi, would you come up to my desk? Class, get started on the problems on page 237 in your workbooks."

Andi walked silently forward. *Keep your cool. Keep your cool, girl. Maybe he'll just assign it for make-up.* As she approached Mr. Wise's desk, mercy seemed to be less and less of a possibility.

"Miss. Bannerman."

That's definitely not good. "Sir?" She squeaked a little higher this time.

"Is this your 'lost' paper?" Mr. Wise asked, producing her homework paper from inside his grade book.

"Oh, yes, sir. You found it! That's good."

"No, Andi. It isn't. I found it lying beside Jeff's paper as he copied from it during second period."

"He was copying it here?"

"Andi!"

"Oh, yeah—sorry, sir."

"Yes, now . . . from what I understand, you were fine with Jeff using your paper for answers for his homework?"

"Um, yes, well . . . sort of, I'm uh—"

"Andi, you're a smart girl, and you must know that this is cheating."

"Well, I was just trying to . . ." She stopped short, realizing that he probably wouldn't buy the "helping a friend" rationale.

"Andi?"

"Yes, sir?"

"Here is your detention slip and a referral to the principal's office; I will be notifying your father and the counselor's office. Cheating will not be tolerated in any way."

Andi's heart hit the floor.

"Andi?"

"Sir?" she answered somewhat irritated. *What more could he have to say?!*

"You just need to make better decisions. That's all."

Andi grabbed her backpack and books. She practically ran from the room and barely made it around the corner when the tears came. She pressed her back into the space between the lockers and felt the tears burn trails down her face. She hated this—hated trying to be cool, hated making stupid mistakes when she knew better, hated seeing the disappointment in Mr. Wise's eyes. He actually liked her and knew she loved math. And she knew her father would be even more disappointed. "What are we going to do with you?" Andi could already hear the question her father had asked so often. And this time, she had no better answer than before.

Andi took a deep breath and went across the hall into the girl's bathroom. Grabbing a paper towel, she dried her cheeks. With a quick drink of water, Andi pulled herself together and headed toward the dreaded principal's office. Carefully she made her way down the hall, trying not to let her tennis shoes squeak on the freshly buffed tiles. She didn't want to attract any looks from the rooms she passed—no use in everyone knowing she was in trouble again.

As she pulled open the heavy door, Andi grimaced at the aroma lingering inside the lemon-yellow office. *Cheap perfume and strong coffee—someone has overdosed on both!* Andi couldn't help the thought. *How can anyone work here?* she wondered. The smells, tears, and stress had given her one whopping headache.

"Miss Bannerman." The lady that worked at the desk looked up.

"Yes, ma'am," Andi answered in her most polite voice.

"Dr. Mitchell is on the phone with your father right now. He'll be with you when he is finished. Until then, just have a seat."

"Yes, ma'am." Andi's eye wandered to the ticking clock. It seemed to move so much slower in the principal's office. *Do they rig them differently just to drive us nuts?* she wondered. Giving up, Andi leaned back against the chair and closed her eyes. *Such a tough Monday . . . and I really wanted it to be a good day.*

Bam! The door to the principal's office swung open and hit the wall behind it. "Andrea Bannerman, come in here."

Andrea? Yep, I'm dead. Andi didn't even look at Dr. Mitchell as she made her way into his office.

"Sit down," he bellowed.

Sitting in a big leather chair, Andi tried to become as small as she could, wishing invisibility was a true option.

"Andi, I just don't know what to say. We do not allow cheating here. You know that. You're a good student, and your so-called "friends" don't need you to do their homework for them. They need to learn it for themselves. And you, Andi, need to make better choices."

Was that the theme of the day or something?! "It wasn't like that, sir," Andi whispered.

"I'm really not concerned with what it was or or wasn't 'like.' It won't happen again—is that clear? You will spend every day after school in detention this week. You will also tutor during study hall three times this week. We can't have anymore of this. Work it out, Andi; you are heading down a tough road, and only you can choose to turn it around."

"Yes, sir." *Detention again—Dad's gonna be really peeved about that! And tutoring? That certainly isn't cool. What a day! I just wanna go home.*

"One more thing, Andi. Mrs. Wellsome wants to see you today before you go home."

"Yes, sir."

3

Getting through the Day

*A*ndi kept her head down and somehow made it through the rest of the day without any more trouble. Since she missed lunch period, she had to shove her PB—no jelly—in her mouth between classes. She chatted with her friends but, for the most part, just zoned out. Luckily, the gang understood her temporary lack of coolness.

Jeff was serving his time in an in-school suspension in the library. By the afternoon, the word was out about the whole incident. In a way, Andi was relieved. At least it meant she didn't have to explain it over and over.

Grabbing her homework, backpack, and jacket, Andi popped into Mrs. Wellsome's office after detention. It was quiet in her office—even the secretary was gone. Andi loved the feel of this room. It was warm and always smelled of old books and flowers. Mrs. Wellsome had been Andi's confidant for the last two years.

"Mrs. Wellsome? Are you here?" Andi called.

"I'm in my office. Come on in, Andi."

Andi walked in and sat down. The office was just like it smelled, warm and fresh. Mrs. Wellsome had a cup of tea in her hand. "Would you like a cup of tea, dear?"

"Sure. Thanks."

"I know: lots of milk and three cubes of sugar. Would you hand me that cup and saucer behind you, please?"

Andi picked up the little green-and-yellow cup and saucer. She always loved these meetings with Mrs. Wellsome. Somehow she always felt better when she left.

"Now, Andi, I hear that you had some trouble this morning. Will you tell me about it?"

Andi nodded and went into the whole account, telling her side of the story.

"So from what you're telling me, you did understand that you were being dishonest from the start."

"Yes, but I was trying to help a friend."

"Trying to help or trying to remain cool?"

"I don't know," Andi muttered. "Maybe both."

"Andi, helping him cheat didn't help him; you know that. It certainly didn't help you. Character is the most important part of a person's actions—not being cool. If you give up on your character, Andi, it's like giving up on you."

Fresh tears welled up in Andi's eyes. Mrs. Wellsome had been there through so much. She literally had held Andi's hands and dried many tears in the two years since Andi's mom died. She was the

one person who Andi could be real with—the only person besides her dad.

"I-I just seem to keep messing up."

"Andi, you can change that. And your dad and I can help. It's all about making—"

"I know. Better choices," Andi interrupted. "It's just not always that easy."

"Yes, I know," Mrs. Wellsome gave a sympathetic smile. "You know what I think, Andi? I think you need a fresh start. Your dad does too. Talk to him, Andi. And remember, he loves you."

"I know."

"Drink your tea, dear. Tomorrow is a new day."

For the next few minutes they just visited and chatted about summer and gardens and vacation— all things that seemed so far away from today.

4

The Impending Doom

After finishing her cup of tea, Andi gave Mrs. Wellsome a hug, grabbed her things, and began her walk home. The streets were busy again, and Andi found some comfort in the familiar buzz of traffic that surrounded her. But even the loudest traffic couldn't drown out the thoughts in Andi's head. At this point, she just wanted to get home and talk to her dad. She dreaded that disappointed look she had seen in his eyes so often lately. And she knew that today's stunt would be the most disappointing of all. She just wanted to get it over with and get on with tomorrow. But Andi didn't even know where to start.

Andi walked briskly up and then down the

steep hills that led toward home. The early morning fog had given way to a cool, blue sky with afternoon warmth. In the bay, the spring and early summer days were much cooler than inland.

At the bottom of the hill, Andi turned onto a row of pastel painted houses. Each house was slightly different, although all had the same bay window overlooking the quaint, little street. Home—no matter how difficult the day, Andi loved to come home.

Andi's dad, Beau Bannerman, was home most days when Andi reached the door. And he was *always* home before Andi when she was detained for a little after-school visit. Andi took a deep breath and opened the door. Quietly, she hung her jacket on the hook in the hall.

"Dad? You home?" Andi slowly climbed the short set of stairs to the living area.

"In here, Andi." She looked over to the brown, leather chair where her dad was sitting.

"Come in and sit down, Andi."

Andi noticed a book in his lap. *Hmm, he's been reading. Maybe he's not as mad as I thought.* Unable to stand the suspense, Andi blurted, "Dad, are you mad? It really isn't as bad as it seems. I talked with Mrs. Wellsome, and she—" The expressionless look on his face was unlike any "Dad look" Andi had seen. "Dad?"

"Andi, I know this isn't going to be easy for you."

"Yeah, I know, but I can do it. See, Jeff isn't really a *bad* guy. Well, he's not really that *smart*, obviously. I mean, can you believe he was copying my work *in math class*? Right in front of Mr. Wise! Anyway, we all make mistakes. I'll try to do better. . . . Dad, are you listening? Dad?"

"Andi, today isn't what I am talking about."

"Oh, it isn't?" Andi giggled nervously. "Well, um, so Dad, what were you talking about?" *I might get out of this easier than I thought!*

"I am talking about all of the trouble you've had this last year."

"Get out of it"? What was I thinking?!

"I know this has been tough on you. It has been tough on both of us since your mom . . . since your mom hasn't been around. We need to make some changes, Andi—some big changes. Now."

"We do?" Andi's eyes grew larger. Somehow she knew these changes were *not* going to be fun.

"Andi, we're moving."

"Moving, we're moving? Where? W-Why?"

"Today was just the breaking point, Andi. Do

you know how hard it is for me to watch my daughter struggle so? I've talked to your principal and Mrs. Wellsome. But I've been thinking about it for some time. For the first time in years, I prayed about it. It is time for a fresh start. We are moving after school gets out."

"Moving! Dad, you can't do that! It isn't fair! What about my friends?! What will I do without my friends?"

"I don't know, Andi, but I'd like to find out." Her dad's voice sounded broken. He sounded so tired.

"That's so cruel, Dad. You never liked my friends, and now you're making me move just to leave them! I thought you were a cool dad. I guess I was wrong."

"I'm not trying to be cool, Andi. Your friends are fine, but the decisions you've made with them, around them, *for* them are not. I can't help but wonder if you're allowing them to negatively influence you."

"What? Dad, I—"

"Enough discussion, Andi. It won't change

anything. We're moving to Delaney Lake right after school is out. We need to start packing immediately—this weekend even."

"Delaney Lake? The . . . the *forest* that we went to in the summers when I was little?! That's, like, five hours away! It's in the boonies! When my friends ask where I'm going, they won't even know where it is! This is so very uncool!"

"Andi, I'm sorry, but the discussion is over."

"I'll be in my room!"

"I think that's a good idea."

Andi charged out of the room and slammed the door. Looking for reassurance, Beau threw an unsure glance toward the ceiling. "I hope You're right," he whispered with a slight smile.

Hours later, Andi lay on her bed in the room that she and her mom had decorated. The slanted eves and dormer windows made it the coziest room ever. Mom had suggested the yellow-and-purple-flowered bedding, saying it would grow with her. (She was always full of practical advice like that.) The walls were Mom's doing as well—light purple on the bottom, with the eves painted a faint yellow. It was warm and fresh, complemented by the breeze of the bay flowing in through the open window. City sounds made their way in also. Cities never seemed to sleep.

Throwing back the comforter, Andi crawled in, hiding in the warmth of the bed. She was exhausted. Would life ever be normal again? She was just starting to feel semi-normal at school, and then—surprise—they're moving! Replaying the discussion—if you could call it that—with her dad, Andi marveled that her father had actually forgotten to punish her. That, she was thankful for. And, deep down, Andi knew that this move wasn't intended to be a punishment—even though it sure felt like it.

What would she tell her friends tomorrow? How could she and her dad leave this house—their home? There was so much "Mom" in this house. How could Dad do this? How *would* they do this?

5

Last Day, Last Night

The last four weeks of school passed without any other big issues. Andi kept up in school and—miraculously—completed the final days without a single detention. (Andi just knew that if she got another detention, they'd move even sooner.)

On the last day of school, Andi gave her final cool performance. "Well, you guys stay out of trouble." Andi forced a smile. "Maybe I'll see ya around."

"Sure thang," Jeff said with a nod. He hadn't been able to look Andi in the eye since the day after the cheating incident when she had told them about the move.

Chapter 5

"Definitely come visit," Tami added.

"Yeah," Abby added.

"Will do—if I can find my way out of Booneyville." With one last look back at her school, Andi waved goodbye and headed home. That was it. Abby had invited her to a sleepover, but what did it matter now? Tomorrow they would live half a day's drive away. She had to get home and finish packing anyway. Tomorrow would be an early start.

That night, Andi and her dad ate take-out from Mr. Wong's, one of their favorite Chinese restaurants. Their beds would be sleeping bags on the floor. They were packed and ready to go.

"Dad, do they have take-out in Delaney Lake?"

"No, honey, I don't think so. But you know

what?" Dad quickly added. "I told you I was buying the old general store to run, right? Maybe we can add some kind of take-out service to our store once we get started."

"Yeah, I guess," Andi mumbled. *What good is take-out if you have to make it yourself?!*

"Well, let's get some sleep. Tomorrow will be a long day."

"I'm expecting that."

"Love you."

"You too."

Andi woke up early the next morning and was ready to go way before her dad had finished his last house check. She walked into her room one last time. "Bye, room, you've been the best room a girl could have." She then added, "Thanks, Mom." At that moment, she turned on one foot and didn't look back.

"Come on, Dad. Let's get it over with."

"Okay, Andi, grab your bag. I'll meet you in the car."

6

The Journey

It was still dark when Andi and her dad started toward their new home. The traffic was lighter than normal, and they made it over the Bay Bridge into the East Bay before the morning rush. The car ride was quiet. Both Andi and her dad were lost in their thoughts. Beau drove east, sipping his Starbucks. Andi munched on a chewy bagel and noisily slurped her O.J. while gazing out the window. The cityscape gave way to busy suburbs, then finally to rolling coastal mountains, windmills, and cows.

"Dad, did you toot?"

Startled, Dad glanced toward Andi and chuckled. "No, did you?"

"Da-ad."

"Andi, it's the cows!"

"Gross!" Andi exclaimed, pinching her nose. "Will it smell like this the whole way?"

"I doubt it. Why don't you lie back and close your eyes for a while?"

"That won't make the smell go away! Besides, I'm not tired. I can't believe we're going to live this far in the boonies. The grass is so brown. It's like the desert out here. I hope Delaney Lake isn't this desolate. I mean, no one lives here! I bet even the cows hate it!"

After a few hours in the car, Beau pulled off the highway into a small town at the base of the Sierra Nevadas. The mountain peaks rose high above the roofs of the small town.

"Is this it? Where's the lake?"

"Andi, this isn't it. Aren't you hungry?"

"Oh, yeah. Guess I forgot. Is it lunchtime already?"

"Um, yeah, as far as I'm concerned it is. These are the best hamburgers in the world! Go to the bathroom, and we'll get a, uh, hamburger brunch."

Beau and Andi gobbled down hamburgers, fries, and shakes and buckled themselves back into their little, green Honda for the last hour of their journey.

"Dad, how far is it now?"

"An hour or so, but this is the prettiest part of the drive."

They drove out of the small town and up into

the foothills. Andi watched out the window as her surroundings grew greener and greener. The scattered scrub oak trees became forests, and then, suddenly pine trees were everywhere.

"Dad, did you see that?"

"What?"

"The trees—all of a sudden they're all pines."

"That's called a tree line. Above 3,000 feet, the pines grow abundantly."

"Three thousand feet above what?"

"Sea level," Dad answered, distracted. He concentrated on the constant curve of the road.

"Three thousand feet above sea level? Above San Francisco? Whoa. . . . Mmm, I love the smell."

"Me too, hon. Me too."

7
We're Home?

ndi rode the rest of the way in silence. The mountains *were* beautiful. She could feel part of her heart melting in this place, but she still wasn't convinced she could really live here. Not that she had any choice.

The car made a hard right, then a left at the fork. Off to the right was a beautiful, blue lake. The road followed the shoreline in and out of several secluded coves. As she and her dad drove above the lake, Andi could see people on the shore and boats skidding across the water. It had been a long time since Andi had been here. The last time her family came here, she was eight years old, long before her life was turned upside-down.

The road led into an itty, bitty town. *This is home?* Andi thought. *Uhhh, where's the mall? What do they do for fun?* Suddenly, the little, green car pulled into a parking space right in front of the dusty front porch of a general store. Her dad practically jumped from the car.

"Andi, we're here!"

"I can see that, Dad."

"I'm just going to run next door to get the key to the house and the store."

"I'll wait in the car," Andi answered, clearly less excited than her dad.

A bell clanged as her dad burst into the real estate office next door. He talked to the lady for what seemed like forever. Finally, he shook her hand and came bursting out the door.

"Grab your stuff, kiddo! Let's go!"

"Uh, where's the house?"

"Right here! Come on! Get moving!"

"Dad! I'm not going to live in the store!"

"We don't live in the store, silly. We own the house *behind* the store. Now, come on, and watch your 'tude!"

Andi followed her dad on the dirt path around the side of the store. Behind the loading area and the big doors was a patch of thick trees. There, Andi followed her dad up the steep path. By the time Andi and her dad reached the top, they were both huffing.

"Guess this country living will get us both in shape." Beau said as he tried to smile between breaths.

"Dad, let's just get there already." Andi followed her dad to the deck of a rather weathered house. It had the shape of an "A" and was made solely out of redwood and windows. There was no paint on the boards. *What happened to the paint? Is this a house or a cabin? This really isn't where we're gonna live is, it?* Andi was careful not to let any of her thoughts slip out.

"Um, Dad?"

"This is it. Welcome home, honey!"

"This is it?" Andi walked along the deck to what seemed to be the front of the house that was really the back of the house, at least from her perspective. Standing out on the deck, Andi realized that this house had one redeeming quality—the view. Beyond the deck was a sandy beach and a beautiful view of the blue water. This would have been amazing, had it not also been so scary. This was her new home.

8

A Mountain of Boxes

---

*A*ndi couldn't believe the dryness she felt in the mountain air. The damp breezes of the bay had been replaced by a constant rustling of pine needles far above her head. Andi was dripping with sweat as she trudged up the path for the last time. Her arms were full of boxes and her shoulder was weighted down with a large duffle bag.

"Dad?"

"In here."

Andi stumbled around the corner and into the kitchen. "This is the last of the stuff, Dad. *Umph*." She set down the boxes and let the duffle bag slide off her shoulder to the floor. "I locked the car," she said, handing her dad the keys.

"Thanks, hon. I don't know if that's even necessary up here," he said with a smile. "So, what do ya think?"

"Well, it's kinda . . . I don't know, Dad. It's sort of . . . it's different than I expected."

"What were you expecting?"

"I don't know. It's just sort of *old*. You know, like no one has lived here for a long time." Andi honestly doubted if anyone had ever lived here, but she didn't point that out. She was just too tired at this point to have an attitude.

"Actually, Andi, no one has ever lived here."

Andi just raised her eyebrows in interest, holding back a giggle.

"This was a vacation home for a family that lived in the valley."

"Really? People thought this home was a vacation? What was their *real* home like?"

"Andi, this home is a great find. It's lakefront, near the store, and doesn't need any real repair, just a little love. That's where we come in. We'll make it home. You'll see."

"Whatever you say, Dad." Andi looked around the very dated cabin. *Just a little love? Yeah, and Einstein was a little smart.* Andi looked back at her father. For the first time in years, he actually looked happy. He looked excited. Not wanting to disappoint him, Andi decided to drop the conversation about the state of the house.

"Dad, I'm gonna look around the house a bit, then I'll start on my room."

"That's fine, Andi. We're gonna eat in about a half hour. Be back down here around 5:30, okay?"

"Okay, Dad. What's for dinner?"

"Weenies and beans. That's mountain talk for chili dogs!"

"Sounds like we're camping."

"Yup. Sounds good, huh?"

"I guess." It did sound good. Andi was starving. *All this hard work really takes a lot out of a girl,* she thought. Andi walked into the front room and looked around. It had dark, paneled walls and brown carpet—definitely an "outdoorsy" feel. In the center of the room was a fireplace with a heavy mantel on it. *Good place to put our family photos,* she thought.

The room was warm and stuffy from being closed up for so long. The back wall had a huge sliding glass door that opened to the back deck. The lake was really beautiful. The sky and trees and clouds were reflected in the waves out on the lake. From the living room, Andi headed up the narrow staircase and peeked in at the first room on the right. Here, Andi found her dad's bed and furniture already in place in the large room. It, too, had a deck that overlooked the lake. *Nice, Dad,* Andi thought. *He even has his own bathroom. That's good for both of us.*

9

A Gift among the Mess

Crossing the hall, Andi found a bathroom that would be hers, a spare room full of office supplies and boxes, and her room. She opened the wood-paneled door and looked inside. It was at the back of the house, away from the lake. The room had a familiar feel. The windows were large and opened, allowing the scent of pine to fill the room. From the open windows came the drifting sounds from the town down the hill.

The movers had already put Andi's bed together and placed her furniture neatly around the room. Her dad had obviously tried to make the most out of the space in the small room. Her boxes and belongings were another story. They were scattered and stacked precariously throughout her room. This would be a major job.

Flopping down onto her bed, Andi looked up at the ceiling. She was exhausted, and the daunting task that waited didn't make it any better. Her legs and back ached. Rolling over, she aimlessly sifted through a small box near her bed. "I don't remember packing this one," she remarked. In the box were trinkets and ribbons and photos. It looked like it belonged to a girl her age, but it still wasn't ringing any bells. "Maybe the movers got this mixed up," she said to herself. "I hope they didn't leave *my* stuff with *this* girl."

"Maybe there's a name in here or something." She picked up a book. "Hey—a journal! Bet there's some good stuff in here!" Opening the front cover, Andi heard the binding crackle. It felt really old. She read the first page aloud. "Jan Howard . . . 1977!! No WAY!!! This was . . . this is Mom's journal from when she was a kid! I can NOT believe it!"

Quickly flipping the pages, Andi noticed that they were all full—full of her mother's thoughts written in a young girl's hand. "Dad! DAD!! DAAA-AAAAD!" Andi yelled as she ran down the stairs.

"Andi? What is it?! Are you okay?" Her dad stopped pouring the mugs of root beer and looked up to see what all of the commotion was about.

"Dad!! I was looking through some boxes, and, well, it didn't even look like it was mine, so I was looking for a name, and then I found this book and—"

"*Whoaaa*, there." Dad chuckled. "Slow down. What's going on?"

Andi took a deep breath and pulled the book

from behind her back. "Dad, do you know what this is? Do you??"

"An old book?"

"Dad! It's Mom's journal!"

"Mom's what?"

"Her journal from when she was a kid, around my age I think."

"Really? Where did you find it?"

"It was in a box in my room. I was sort of unpacking and just found it! Can you believe it? Can you?!"

In disbelief, Beau slowly opened the journal. Looking down at the name and dates, he skimmed a few entries. "I . . . I didn't know we had these. Your mom told me that she had kept a journal when she was a kid, but I had no idea. . . . What an awesome gift you've found, Andi." Beau looked up and handed the journal back to his daughter.

Andi's dad didn't look up, but she noticed his lashes were wet. She didn't want him to hurt anymore, but she had to ask, "Dad, would it bother you if I read it? It would really mean a lot to me."

"Not at all, Andi. It's yours. I knew that was some of your mom's stuff, but I had no idea it held her journals. I put it with your things so that you would have a part of your mom with you in your new room. I guess now you do." Beau stopped and smiled thoughtfully. "I'd love to hear about it as you read it. When you're finished, I'd like to read it too."

"Thanks, Dad. I can't wait! Let's eat, huh?"

Amazed at his child's ability to move from such a tender moment straight to food, Beau chuckled to himself and began serving the chili dogs. They spent the rest of the evening chatting and trying to make some headway with the boxes in the kitchen. By 9:00, Andi and her dad were both beat. "Okay, that's enough for one day," he announced. "The boxes will still be here tomorrow."

"That's what I'm afraid of," Andi sighed with a slight grin.

Beau made his rounds in their new home, locking the doors and turning off the lights.

"Wait, Dad! Leave on the stair light, please. It is really black in here with no lights on."

"That's country living." Beau put his arm around Andi and nudged her up the stairs. "Do you want help making up your bed?"

"Nah, Dad. I'll just grab a cover and crash."

"Okay, call me when you're ready. Don't forget your headgear."

Ugh, headgear! Why do I still need to wear that anyway? It's not like there are people here I'll wanna impress with my supermodel teeth anyway. Andi brushed her hair and teeth, strapped on her head-gear, and found an old night shirt in her things. She was in her bed in record time and was fast asleep even before her dad came to tuck her in. The old journal lay on her desk, waiting for a time when its new owner could stay awake long enough to enjoy it.

10

Good Morning

---

ndi turned over in bed, trying to catch those last few moments of precious sleep. She stretched, squirmed, and then pulled the pillow tightly over her face. The sun was streaming in through the dormer window, catching particles of dust floating on the beams. The birds outside were obviously awake and trying to make sure that every neighbor within earshot was too. The green numbers on the clock admitted that it was barely 7:00.

Andi stretched one last time, took out her headgear, and swung her long legs onto the rough wood floor. In from the window came a morning breeze and the smells of coffee, fire, and bacon.

Andi took a moment to look around her attic room — the slanted roof, the nice, fluffy bed, and the many, *many* boxes cluttering the space. *It might turn out okay—even if it is in the boonies,* Andi thought.

After throwing on her UCLA sweatshirt and a pair of jeans, she stuck a headband in her long, dark hair, flung her bag over her shoulder, and headed for the door. Turning to take one last look at the mess, Andi retrieved the journal lying on her desk and threw it into her bag. She bounded down the stairs, with the intention of exploring the lake before her dad grabbed her for more unpacking.

Breathless, Andi reached the last stair, with freedom just a few steps beyond her reach. *Squeeaaak!* "Agh! What is it with these old steps?" Andi muttered.

"What's that, hon? Wow! You're up early!" her dad said, slowly emerging from his room and heading toward the kitchen.

"Yeah, well, with all the racket . . ." Andi motioned toward the window.

"Racket? Sounds like a symphony compared to the mornings in the city." Beau smiled. "You know, you haven't been up this early on a Saturday since your were my 'early shiner.'" He patted her head as he went for the coffee.

"Dad! Can we not talk about my baby days today?"

"Oh yeah, yeah. I forgot. We're cool, right? So, what do cool girls eat for breakfast? Let's see . . . not quite ready for coffee, right? How about some Lucky Charms?"

"*Humph*, well, I really don't like breakfast," Andi said, not finding the "cool" joke very humorous.

He couldn't understand how hard it was to try to fit in, how important it was to be, well, *cool*.

Andi's dad handed her a bowl of cereal and together they sat at the olive-green Formica . . . and munched in harmony. "Honey, what are your plans? You are planning to unpack your room, riiiight?"

"Dad, I will. I promise, but can I explore just a little first?"

"Andi, we have so much to do. This house has got to be livable by Monday, and the store opens next week. We have so much to accomplish between now and then."

Andi looked around. *I doubt this house will ever be livable with its out-of-date décor and all of our junk everywhere.* But wanting to keep the peace and gain some early morning freedom, Andi kept that thought to herself. Instead, she chose the more mature approach. "Dad, pleeeeeeease!" she begged. "I'll be back before you get through the paper—promise!"

Beau looked at Andi, then at the bewildering mess, and admitted to himself that a little walk

might do her good. "Okay, but remember, this paper is a bit thinner than the one I'm used to in the city."

Andi started to roll her eyes but thought better of it, kissed her dad's cheek, and ran for the deck door. "Be back soon!" she yelled as the screen door slammed behind her.

11

The Meeting

ndi stopped a second to look at the lake before she headed down the stairs toward the path to the shore. *Wow—you can see so much from up here*, she thought. *The lake looks like a mirror this time of day. I guess I can see why my dad calls this place paradise; I'm just not sure I can live here. Does anyone really live here?*

When she reached the end of the path, Andi stood at the shore. She picked up a rock and threw it into the lake, watching the circles ripple out in all directions. Andi chose her rocks very carefully at first, keeping some in her pocket to take back home. Before long, she was lobbing hefty rocks far into the lake. The big *ker-plunks* amused her, as she heaved

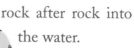

rock after rock into the water.

Eying a target, Andi picked up a smooth stone the size of her fist, wound up, and aimed for the fallen log floating toward the middle of the lake.

Just as she released the rock, something cracked behind her and tumbled. Andi spun around in mid-stroke, ready to defend herself from the suspect animal, and threw the rock into the air. Oh, if only it weren't headed directly toward a really cute guy.

Smack! Unfortunately, it was a perfect shot, hitting Mr. Cute Guy squarely in the gut.

"Oh, no. Oh, goodness. Oh, my. Oh, I'm so sorry. Ohhh, are you okay?!"

"Yeah . . . I think I—I think I just got the wind knocked out of me. Got to sit down."

"Oh, oh, I'm really, really sorry. Oh, no. Oh—"

"Can you stop saying that?"

"Oh, sorry."

"Just stop. I'm okay." He brushed off his T-shirt and jeans and tussled his hair with his fingers.

Andi observed that his hair was a bit longer than she cared for on a guy, but then again, it did have sort of an edgy look. At that moment, he looked up at Andi, totally busting her during the hair analysis. He insecurely tried to straighten it once more. "Are you the new kid that just moved in at the store?"

"Um, yeah. I'm Andi. 'Andi' with an 'i' because it's a girl's name. I mean, of course it's a girl's name. It's *my* name. I'm a girl. Well, anyway, nice to meet you."

"Thanks for clearing that up." The boy

smirked. "I'm Mitch. You always throw rocks at innocent guys out taking morning walks?"

"I didn't know it was you. I mean, I thought you were a . . . I mean, sorry."

"Yeah, yeah. I told you, I'm okay. Really, I am." He glanced back toward the path. "Well, I'd better get going. Nice to meet you too—I think."

"See ya." Andi watched as Mitch picked up his pencil and pad and walked toward the path. "Hey, what were you doing sneaking up on me anyway?" Andi called, in an effort to recover from her embarrassment.

"Sneaking? Nah, I always come here to draw in the morning, before the lake gets too busy with skiers and all."

"To draw?"

"Yeah. See ya."

"See ya!"

12

A Word from Mom

So much has happened, and it's not even 8:00 in the morning! Andi thought. This place is certainly not as boring as I thought. Andi sat on a rock and looked at the lake. He draws. . . . Wow, this must be a great thinking spot if he walks all the way here just to draw.

Gazing out at the first of the boats hitting the water, Andi smiled at the families readying for a day on the lake. She watched one little boat piled high with all the ingredients of a fun-filled lake trip: water skis, a red cooler, overflowing grocery bags, brightly colored beach towels, and an eager little girl sitting stiffly in her life jacket. As the little boat gained speed, Andi watched the mother dive to

catch a towel that began to topple at the top of the tower.

Andi smiled and remembered her mom. She wished she still had her to talk to. Then she remembered. "The journal!" she exclaimed, a little too loudly. The trees rustled as startled birds flew from the branches. "Payback!" she yelled, smiling up at her early morning neighbors.

Andi reached into the bag and opened the journal. Ceremoniously, Andi read the first page aloud. "Jan's Journal. September 1977. Age 11." Andi closed the book and, for a moment, pondered whether or not to keep reading. But desperately needing a glimpse of her mom, Andi opened to the first entry:

September 10, 1977

Dear Journal,

Ugh. Today I am starting a new school. I didn't even want to move to C.A. Dad said we had no choice; his job was making him move. Can they even do that? The school I am going to is B-I-G, BIG. I am sure the kids all know each other. What if I have no one to eat lunch with? I always thought the lonely lunch kids were so sad, and now it might be me! Mom said not to worry — something about Jesus watching out for me and providing for all my needs and something about the sparrows in the field. I'm not sure I know what that has to do with eating lunch.

Anyway got to go.

Love,
Me (Jan)

September 10, 1977

Dear Journal,

Got to write fast cause it's late. But had to write quickly about my day! We switch classes here in 6th grade. On my way to math, I wasn't watching where I was going and smacked into a girl (embarrassing!) but she was really nice. Her name is Sherry. She likes to dance and likes math, can't spell. We think a lot alike. Anyway, she invited me to eat lunch with her. Boy, was I relieved! It was just before lunch. I told mom and she reminded me that God did provide. Still not sure about the sparrow thing, but he did provide. That much sure is true.

Thanks God!

Love,
Me

Andi closed the journal and looked up to the clouds. *Do You really provide like that, God? Did You for my mom? Wait! Sherry? Aunt Sherry? She always said she isn't really my aunt, but I call her that 'cause she and Mom were so close. Wow! Guess He does provide. Please, God, provide friends here for me.*

Andi stood up and dusted the dirt from her jeans. *Hmm, maybe God is already taking care of me. Maybe He helped me find this journal. And maybe, just maybe, He introduced me to Mitch. . . . Maybe.*

13
Lunch Meetings

---

*A*ndi noticed the sun rising higher in the sky and realized that the morning was getting away from her. She quickly turned back to hike up the path toward home. By the time she reached the upper deck, she was sweating something awful. She couldn't believe how hot it got so early in the day.

Before charging through the side door, Andi stopped long enough to examine the constant rustling coming from above her head—the pines. She looked up to see little streams of light shining down through the pine trees on her. *This may be the boonies, but it's definitely beautiful.*

Tucking the journal under her arm, she rushed up the stairs to put it away, not quite ready to discuss her thoughts. *These jeans have got to go!* Andi thought, throwing off her jeans and digging for a pair of shorts.

Leaping back down the stairs, Andi found her dad in the front room.

"Hey, Dad, I'm back."

"There you are. I was beginning to think you had gotten lost. I had to read the paper three times," he joked. "See anything interesting?"

"Um, define 'interesting.'"

"Pirate ships? Buried treasure?" her dad asked with exaggerated excitement.

"In that case, no." Andi grinned at her dad. "So, what's first?"

"I guess start with your bedroom and bathroom. Unpack all your things and put them away. Neatly, Andi. Just throw your boxes down the stairs when you're done. I'll fold them and take them to the—"

"Dad, are we gonna unpack all day?" she interrupted. "This is so boring."

"I guess that's up to you." Beau raised his eyebrows into that fatherly look. "It doesn't have to be all day, if you move quickly. I've already finished the kitchen, and the living room is my next job. You should be able to finish your bed and bathroom before lunch." Her dad turned back toward a full box. "I'd like to take you to lunch at The Cove, if we finish soon enough."

"What's 'The Cove'?"

"It's a neat little restaurant that overlooks the marina. We can even eat outside, and the menu is definitely better than those weenies and beans."

"Sounds great. I'm already starved! I'll finish my room quickly so I'll have time for a shower before we go. It is so hot up here!"

"Oh, you'll get used to it. Now let's get going. I'm hungry too."

Andi grabbed a snack and then headed up the stairs. The boxes in her room seemed to have grown since she last saw them. *Might as well get started,* she thought, mustering the discipline to open the first box. As she went through the clothes boxes, she hung her clothes neatly in the closet and then organized her drawers in her room. It was nice to put things back in order. It helped to make it feel like home. *At least here I know where everything is,* she thought. *Well, for now anyway.*

Andi made it through her desk and dresser knick-knacks in no time. On the top shelf of her organized closet, she delicately placed the box of her mom's belongings. Just knowing that the box held old photos and more journals, Andi felt closer to her mom. On her nightstand, Andi gently placed her favorite photo of a much younger Andi with her mom and dad. Beside it she put a small photo of her friends back home and the journal that she was reading.

In the last and largest box, Andi found all of her old bedding and matching bathroom apparel. *Yes! This should go fast!* she thought. In no time, the box was empty—pillows on the bed and bathmats on the floor. Turning around for the final impression, Andi was amazed at how good it looked and how much it felt like home. The cream walls perfectly enveloped her yellow and purple bedding. The yellow and purple rag mats really helped to brighten the small bathroom. The flowery décor almost seemed more at home here, away from the city.

Feeling a sense of accomplishment—and an even stronger sense of hunger—Andi quickly threw the boxes down the stairs to her dad.

"Look out below!"

"Done already?" her shocked dad called from below.

"Yes, sir! I'm jumping in the shower and will be down in five."

"Okay! I'll be ready too."

Andi grabbed her stuff and headed for the shower. It seemed to take forever for the water to get warm! Andi jumped in and out of the shower, combed her hair, and again pulled it back in a headband. Looking in the mirror, she couldn't believe how much she'd changed in the last few months. She was really growing up. She didn't look like a little girl anymore . . . and she was certainly thankful for that.

Grabbing the towel from the floor and flinging it on the hook, Andi left the room and leapt down the stairs. "Dad, let's go. I'm starved."

"Keys . . . keys. Okay, here they are. Let's go."

Heading down the dirt path to the town below, Andi sputtered at the dust that attacked her while she tried to follow her dad.

"Is it always—*puh!*—this dusty?"

"I think it is most days. Dusty or muddy or icy in the winter."

"Wow. You sure make it sound incredible," Andi replied dryly.

"Just give it a chance, sweetie. You'll like it. It'll just take time."

"Well, I guess I've got plenty of that." Andi lowered her voice to a murmur. "And plenty of dust all over my legs. *Why* did I shower?"

Obviously preoccupied with the smell of food, her dad called, "Here we are."

The two newcomers walked into a rustic wood cabin restaurant. The walls were all opened beam. The place seemed pretty dark, with lanterns on the tables. It wasn't fancy dark, just dark-dark. The hostess led them through the restaurant to the back door. They all stepped out onto the deck. The direct sunlight and its reflection off the water were so bright that it took Andi a few minutes to adjust.

"This okay, sir?" the hostess asked.

"This is great, huh, Andi?" her dad asked.

"Yeah." Andi squinted. "I'm just a little blind."

"Andi, have a seat," Beau prompted.

"What? Okay, thanks." Andi bumped into the table almost sending the lantern—unlit, thankfully—flying off the table.

The hostess steadied the lantern, studying Andi closely. "Your waitress will be right with you," she said.

"Thanks," Beau said, then turned to his daughter. "Andi, you okay?"

"Yeah, it's just so bright." Andi wiped her eyes and felt her red cheeks. "How embarrassing," she said. For once, she was thankful no one knew her here.

"I'm gonna get the fish sandwich. What do you want?"

"A cheeseburger, plain, fries, and can I have a Coke?"

"You have to ask? How old are you?" he chided.

Just then, Andi looked up and saw a girl about her age holding an order pad. Add another red-faced embarrassment to the pile.

"Hi. I'm Daphne Delaney, your waitress for today. My dad owns the place. Actually, he owns a lot of this lake area. His regular waitress is out with a cold." The girl rolled her eyes. "I'm just helping out. A little boring, really, but a great way to make some fast cash. So what do you want?"

"Hi there, Daphne. I'm Beau Bannerman—"

Oh, no, Dad, don't, please—

"And this is my daughter, Andi."

Great. Now she knows exactly who the clumsy, bumbling, I-have-to-ask-my-daddy-if-I-can-order-a-Coke girl is.

"We just moved here."

"Oh, I heard you were coming. From the city, right?" She turned to Andi. "And you'll be a seventh grader in the fall, won't you? Me too! Maybe we can hang, you know? Hey! I could show you around later if you want."

Andi looked at Daphne and was somewhat relieved. Obviously the previous antics hadn't scared her too badly. Plus, she reminded Andi a lot of the girls in San Francisco. She was stylish and pretty. She even seemed pretty friendly.

"Um, that would be nice," Andi said, recovering from her embarrassment. "I'll have to see."

"You have to ask your dad about *that* too?" she quickly replied.

Okay, back to the red cheeks.

"I don't have to ask anymore. I just tell my parents what I'm doing out of courtesy." Daphne Delaney smiled proudly.

Andi's mouth almost fell open at that one. Even her friends in San Francisco were smart enough not to talk like that in front of a parent.

"Yeah, well, I'll see," Andi said eying her dad. "Anyway, I'll have a cheeseburger, fries, and a Coke."

"I'll have the fish sandwich and a salad, ranch dressing," Beau said.

"Okay, I'll get that going right away. And let me know if I can do anything further to help. I like good tips." Daphne smiled and sauntered down the patio.

When she was out of earshot, Andi leaned toward her dad. "Sooo, can I hang out with Daphne later?"

He paused. "I'm not sure she's what you need

in a friend, Andi."

"Aw, come on, Dad! You don't even know her! Her family is obviously a big part of the community here. How many girls my age do you think live here?"

"You have a point. I guess seeing the area with her today is fine." Her dad then added cautiously, "But if we have any trouble, Andi, it's over. You won't hang out with her if she is a problem for you. Do you understand?"

"Thanks, Dad! You're the greatest!" Andi was thrilled to have made a cool friend already. But then again, she couldn't shake the feeling that maybe this wasn't the exact friend she had prayed for.

Lunch was finished without further embarrassment thankfully. Andi was starved, and the food was good. Before getting up to leave, Andi made plans to meet Daphne back at the restaurant later in the day.

This could be good, she thought, walking back into the dark restaurant toward the front doors.

14

Bumping into a Friend

The candlelight in the restaurant didn't really help Andi make her way to the front door. Just as she reached the hostess station at the front of the restaurant, Andi turned and ran directly into the chest of a very large man. Jumping back—and noting embarrassment number three—Andi said, "Oh, excuse me, sir, I . . . I was trying to get to the door. I . . . my eyes are still adjusting to the light, or rather, the lack of light."

"No worries, little one," the kind man stated in a husky voice. "I am Pastor Ed Jacoby, from the Community Church up on the hill. You're the new family that owns the little store on the corner, am I right?" He shook Beau's hand, then offered his large

hand to Andi.

"Yes, we are the Bannermans. This is my daughter, Andi, and I'm Beau. So nice to meet you."

"It's lovely to meet you folks. This is my daughter, Ellie. I think she's about your age, Andi. Ellie will be in the seventh grade this fall. Andi, what about you?"

Andi looked at the friendly face of Ellie. She was tall and sort of gangly. She had her father's kind smile. Her face was pretty but hidden behind a set of very large glasses.

"Hi, Andi, Mr. Bannerman. So nice to meet you both. I am so glad you're here. We can sure use a new girl in our grade." She took a quick breath. "You dress really cool. Do you shop in the city? Well, of course you did. That's where you lived, right? I do like your clothes. We have some nice malls down in the valley. I'm sure you'll like them too." She was very friendly but spoke so fast that Andi had a hard time keeping up.

"It's nice to meet you too, Ellie. I am glad to hear there are shops nearby. I was beginning to wonder where the mall was."

"Yeah, hee-hee. We *do* have a mall." She put on an exaggerated drawl. "Even us mountain girls like to shop."

Andi liked Ellie instantly. She seemed warm and confident and fun. She wasn't as serious as a lot of her friends back home.

Andi noticed Daphne standing over in the corner with her arms crossed, watching the entire encounter with a menacing stare. She wasn't sure what the stare was about, but it made her ready to get out of there.

At Ellie's next pause, Andi looked up at her dad. "Well, Dad, we need to get going. We still have lots of work to do at home."

"You're right, hon," he said, giving her a surprised glance. "We do need to go. It was great to meet you both."

"Hey, Andi, would you want to meet me for Sunday school tomorrow? We could meet on the steps, and I'll show you around."

"Um, thanks, but we don't normally go to—"

"We'd love to join you for service tomorrow," Dad chimed in. Andi and her dad hadn't stepped foot in a church since her mom's funeral. "I really feel that it is time to go back, for a number of reasons,"

Beau added, giving Andi a don't-question-me-about-this look.

"Why don't you and Andi meet us on the front steps at nine o'clock? The girls can go their way, and we'll go to Bible study. Then, we'll meet up with the kids for the service," Pastor Jacoby suggested.

"Sounds great." Beau smiled at the man and his daughter. "We'll see you in the morning."

"Bye, Andi, nice to meet you."

"You too, Ellie."

"See you tomorrow." Ellie gave a small wave.

"See ya," Andi said and turned to leave. She noticed Daphne was still watching the four of them. Correction, she was *glaring* at the four of them. *Wonder what's up with her,* Andi thought. *Why is she so bothered by us talking with the Jacobys? They seem like really nice folks.*

On the way home Andi and her dad talked about all they wanted to get accomplished that afternoon before she was to meet up with Daphne. Arriving at the cabin, Andi sunk into a chair and muttered, "We still have a lot to do, don't we?"

"Yup, let's just get to it. Sooner we're done, the sooner we can relax a bit," Andi's dad said. "If you're gonna meet up with Daphne, we need to kick it in high gear."

"Dad? Are you okay with me meeting Daphne?"

"Well," he began, "that depends on how you act when you are with Daphne and what type of friend Daphne turns out to be. I'm okay with you going today, but I do have some concerns."

"Dad, I'll stay clear of trouble. You can trust me."

"I am counting on that, Andi."

"Thanks, Dad. And I'll get going on this mess." Andi turned and began unpacking the remaining boxes downstairs.

15

Getting the Scoop

That afternoon, Andi finished unpacking the boxes and ran upstairs to change her clothes. She was amazed at how hot and dusty she had become in just a few hours. After grabbing a pair of jean shorts and a designer tee, Andi went into her bathroom to freshen up. She wanted to look her best for her afternoon hanging with Daphne. Andi knew that outward appearances would be important to this new friend.

After one more hair check, Andi headed down the stairs, kissed her dad on the cheek, and headed for the door.

"Bye, Dad. What time do I need to be back?" Andi asked.

"Be home by 4:30. And Andi," he said looking directly at his daughter, "be on time."

"Okay. That gives me an hour and a half. Thanks, Dad," Andi yelled over her shoulder, passing through the screen door. Andi wandered down the path and navigated through the trees toward town. Behind her, Andi could hear boats, jet skis, and laughter coming up from the lake. In front of her, she could hear the murmur of the busy little town below. *Seems to be more people here than I thought,* Andi noticed.

As she headed into town, she saw Daphne sitting on the bench outside of The Cove.

"Hey, Andi," Daphne called as Andi approached.

"Hi."

"You want to get an ice cream before we head out?" Daphne offered.

"Sure. I could use a cold treat. Lead the way."

"Cool. My dad owns the ice cream stand down at the marina. Let's walk down there and get one. There're a lot of people to see down there too. All of the boats come in there to get gas and stuff."

"Sounds perfect." Andi smiled. "Let's go."

"Do you need to ask your daddy first?" Daphne said in a sing-songy voice.

Andi gave a nervous laugh. "No, uh, my dad would be fine with this." Andi remembered that her father had told her to stay in town and be home on time. Andi was glad that, for the moment, she appeared to have as much freedom as Daphne. In an effort to change the subject, Andi asked, "This place is really busy. Is it always like this?"

Daphne put her hand across her forehead to shield her eyes from the bright sun coming off the lake. "Yeah, it's really hopping from mid-June through Labor Day. But after that, it's dead. Totally dead. No one is here but the locals."

"Oh, I guess it gets really boring then."

"Not really—at least, no more boring than *now*. Most of the local kids hang out together, no matter what the season. I'm different, of course, 'cause in the summer, I meet a ton of vacationing families and their kids through my dad. My dad owning most of the commercial space in town has some benefits, you know?" She smiled smugly. "Like meeting really cool kids. *They* know how to have fun. Who knows? I might introduce you to some of them this summer—if you're lucky."

By this time, Andi and Daphne had arrived at the ice cream stand. The sun was beating down unmercifully. Andi was so thirsty.

"I'll have a single chocolate mint in a cone," Daphne said in a superior tone.

"Thank you, Daphne," said the woman behind the counter. "What can I get you, miss?"

"I think I'll have a strawberry slush, please," Andi said.

The lady behind the counter moved quickly to get their order. Andi was so hot she couldn't wait to get a sip of her drink. Andi looked over at Daphne. Daphne was sweating too, but didn't seem to notice. *I guess she's used to it. Come to think of it, she*

was more concerned with watching what was happening at the dock than anything else.

"Here're your treats, girls," the lady said, handing them their orders.

"Thank you, ma'am," Andi replied and dug in her pocket to pay for the slush.

"C'mon, Andi. Dad'll cover it." Daphne pulled Andi away from the counter. "Let's go sit at the end of the dock and eat."

Andi turned back to smile at the woman behind the counter and then followed Daphne down the dock. The dock rocked with each passing set of waves, making it difficult to walk straight. But Daphne didn't even waver, her experience making her oblivious to the constant motion of the wooden planks.

After finding a spot at the end of the dock, both girls took their flip flops off and dangled their feet in the water. The water was cool and refreshing. "So what do you think of our little end of 'paradise'?" Daphne asked sarcastically.

"Actually, I think I like it here. I just miss home. It is beautiful here, though. You don't seem to like it much. Am I right?" Andi asked, hoping to find out why Daphne always had such a 'tude.

"I don't know—never lived anywhere else. I just don't fit in. I need excitement. I need people."

"But there are people here . . . like Ellie Jacoby." Andi continued to fish for information. "She seemed friendly enough."

"Ellie? Ugh, don't get me started. She and I, well, we just don't get along. Never have. She's so goody-goody."

"Oh," Andi said, not sure where to go from there. "So you two don't hang out much, huh?"

"Not by choice, anyway. Unfortunately, we do see each other a lot. Ellie's involved in almost everything around here. I am too, but for different reasons."

"So do you go to church with her?"

"Yeah, I go, but only because my dad makes me. He said it makes a good impression on the community for us all to go to church. I just sort of go and sit. You go?"